CLIFFHANGERS 3

Sue Palmer
Alison Kilpatrick
Patricia McCall

Oliver & Boyd

Acknowledgments

The authors and publishers are grateful to the following for permission to reproduce extracts from copyright works:

Blackie & Son Ltd, from *Conrad's War* by Andrew Davies; The Bodley Head, from *The Eighteenth Emergency* by Betsy Byars; Jonathan Cape Ltd, from *Danny The Champion of the World* by Roald Dahl and *Run for your Life* by David Line; Chatto & Windus Ltd, from *Fish* by Alison Morgan; Victor Gollancz Ltd, from *The White Horse Gang* by Nina Bawden; Hamish Hamilton Ltd, from *Space Hostages* by Nicholas Fisk; Macmillan, London and Basingstoke, from *Which Witch?* by Eva Ibbotson and *The Ogre Downstairs* by Diana Wynne Jones; and Penguin Books, from *Me and My Million* by Clive King (Kestrel Books 1976, pp. 20–23, © Clive King 1976).

The authors would also like to thank the children and staff of Comiston Primary School, Edinburgh; Caddonfoot Primary School, Galashiels and Stenwood Elementary School, Virginia, USA, for all their help; and Jeannette Perry, Ishbel Fraser and Graham Harding, without whom *Cliffhangers* could not have been written.

Illustrated by Nancy Bryce, Peter Chapel, Donald Harley and John Harrold

Oliver & Boyd
Robert Stevenson House
1–3 Baxter's Place
Leith Walk
Edinburgh EH1 3BB

A Division of Longman Group Ltd

First published 1983
Second impression 1985

ISBN 0 05 003633 5

Printed in Hong Kong by
Sheck Wah Tong Printing Press Ltd.

Contents

Introduction

In *Cliffhangers* you will find extracts from ten exciting fiction books written for people of your age. There are many sorts of fiction – adventure stories, fantasy, stories set in the past or in other parts of the world, school stories, science fiction – something for everybody to enjoy. We hope that in the *Cliffhanger* extracts, and the sections called "Other Good Reads", you will find many books that you'd like to read for yourself. The "Other Good Reads" are coded with stars – one star means that it is quite an easy read, two means that it is of medium difficulty, and three stars means that it's better left to good readers. Choose books that you know you'll be able to read quite easily – then you can relax and enjoy the story. If you like a book, then it's a good idea to look for other books by the same author.

Sometimes you may be able to find the books you want in your class or school library. If not, the local lending library might have them. You can join the library by going along with an adult and asking for a membership application form. It won't cost you anything! Fiction books are arranged on library shelves alphabetically by authors' surnames. If you can't find the book, then usually it is possible to reserve it and collect it as soon as it is returned, or else the librarian can borrow it from another library. However, since all the *Cliffhanger* extracts come from paperbacks, you may want to buy them – they are fairly cheap.

Most big bookshops have children's sections where you can buy Puffins and other paperbacks. There is even a Puffin Club you can join, which sends you details of the books published in Puffin and a magazine about books. Ask at your bookshop for details of this club.

Often you get more enjoyment from a book if you think about it and talk about it. You may even gain a better understanding of your own thoughts, feelings and experiences when you come across something similar in books. The discussions you are asked to take part in after each extract should help you to understand both the events and the reasons why the characters behave as they do. You will also have the chance to talk about your own experiences and your own thoughts on various subjects connected with the extracts. There is rarely any "right" or "wrong" answer. Your opinions and the way you express them are what counts. Often you get ideas from what other people say, so remember that it is important to listen as well as to speak.

The reading, talking and activities in *Cliffhangers* should all be enjoyable, so have fun and Good Reading!

1 Danny the Champion of the World

by Roald Dahl

Roald Dahl was born in Wales. During the Second World War he was a fighter pilot in the RAF. He has written lots of books — some for children and some for adults. Roald Dahl is married to an actress called Patricia Neal and they have four children.

* * * * * * * * * * * *

Danny's mother died when he was a baby, and ever since then he has lived with his father.

Danny's father is the best fun in the world, and he and Danny have a lovely time together, living in a gypsy caravan and running a filling-station out in the country.

Then one night Danny discovers his father's deep, dark secret. . . .

For some reason I woke up again during the night. I lay still, listening for the sound of my father's breathing in the bunk above mine. I could hear nothing. He wasn't there, I was certain of that. This meant that he had gone back to the workshop to finish a job. He often did that after he had tucked me in.

I listened for the usual workshop sounds, the little clinking noises of metal against metal or the tap of a hammer. They always comforted me tremendously, those noises in the night, because they told me my father was close at hand.

But on this night, no sound came from the workshop. The filling-station was silent.

I got out of my bunk and found a box of matches by the sink. I struck one and held it up to the funny old clock that hung on the wall above the kettle. It said ten past eleven.

I went to the door of the caravan. "Dad," I said softly. "Dad, are you there?"

No answer.

There was a small wooden platform outside the caravan door, about four feet above the ground. I stood on the platform and gazed around me.

"Dad!" I called out. "Where are you?"

Still no answer.

In pyjamas and bare feet, I went down the caravan steps and crossed over to the workshop. I switched on the light. The old car we had been working on through the day was still there, but not my father.

I have already told you he did not have a car of his own, so there was no question of his having gone for a drive. He wouldn't have done that anyway. I was sure he would never willingly have left me alone in the filling-station at night.

In which case, I thought, he must have fainted suddenly from some awful illness or fallen down and banged his head.

I would need a light if I was going to find him. I took the torch from the bench in the workshop.

I looked in the office. I went around and searched behind the office and behind the workshop.

I ran down the field to the lavatory. It was empty.

"Dad!" I shouted into the darkness. "Dad! Where are you?"

I ran back to the caravan. I shone the light into his bunk to make absolutely sure he wasn't there.

He wasn't in his bunk.

I stood in the dark caravan and for the first time in my life I felt a touch of panic. The filling-station was a long way from the nearest farmhouse. I took the blanket from my bunk and put it round my shoulders. Then I went out the caravan door and sat on the platform with my feet on the top step of the ladder. There was a new moon in the sky and across the road the big field lay pale and deserted in the moonlight. The silence was deathly.

I don't know how long I sat there. It may have been one hour. It could have been two. But I never dozed off. I wanted to keep listening all the time. If I listened very carefully I might hear something that would tell me where he was.

Then, at last, from far away, I heard the faint tap-tap of footsteps on the road.

The footsteps were coming closer and closer.

Tap . . . tap . . . tap . . . tap . . .

Was it him? Or was it somebody else?

I sat still, watching the road. I couldn't see very far along it. It faded away into a misty moonlit darkness.

Tap . . . tap . . . tap . . . tap . . . came the footsteps.

Then out of the mist a figure appeared.

It was him!

I jumped down the steps and ran on to the road to meet him.

"Danny!" he cried. "What on earth's the matter?"

"I thought something awful had happened to you," I said.

He took my hand in his and walked me back to the caravan in silence. Then he tucked me into my bunk. "I'm so sorry," he said. "I should never have done it. But you don't usually wake up, do you?"

"Where did you go, Dad?"

"You must be tired out," he said.

"I'm not a bit tired. Couldn't we light the lamp for a little while?"

My father put a match to the wick of the lamp hanging from the ceiling and the little yellow flame sprang up and filled the inside of the caravan with pale light. "How about a hot drink?" he said.

"Yes, please."

He lit the paraffin burner and put the kettle on to boil.

"I have decided something," he said. "I am going to let you in on the deepest darkest secret of my whole life."

I was sitting up in my bunk watching my father.

"You asked me where I had been," he said. "The truth is I was up in Hazell's Wood."

"Hazell's Wood!" I cried. "That's miles away!"

"Six miles and a half," my father said. "I know I shouldn't have gone and I'm very, very sorry about it, but I had such a powerful yearning ... " His voice trailed away into nothingness.

"But why would you want to go all the way up to Hazell's Wood?" I asked.

He spooned cocoa powder and sugar into two mugs, doing it very slowly and levelling each spoonful as though he were measuring medicine.

"Do you know what is meant by poaching?" he asked.

* * * * * * * * * * * *

A. Talking about the story

1. What is meant by "poaching"?

2. What are the signs that tell Danny that his father is nowhere around?

3. Do you think Danny and his father are rich or poor? Why?

B. Talking around the story

1. Poaching is a crime. What other crimes can you think of?
   What do you think is the most serious crime?
   How are people punished for the crimes you have mentioned?
   Have any crimes happened in your area that you know about?

2. Danny and his father are very close to each other. They like to be together and enjoy each other's company.
   Most people have one particular relation or friend that they feel specially close to. Sometimes it is a parent or grandparent, sometimes a brother or sister, or a friend from school.

Who is the person you feel closest to? Why do you
think this is?
What makes a good friend?

C. Activity: interviewing a younger child

In Book 2 of *Cliffhangers*, you were asked to interview a
member of your own class. Today you are going to
interview a younger child from another class about his
or her "best friends".

First you must think out your questions and write them
down. Here are some ideas:
>   Who are your best friends?
>   How long have you known them?
>   How did you meet them?
>   Why do you like them so much?
Make up more questions, but take care to avoid too many
questions where the answer is just "yes" or "no".

Discuss the questions and how to conduct the interview
with your teacher. Practise asking the questions with a
friend.

If you are going to write the answers down, remember to
take pencil and paper. If you are going to use a tape-
recorder, make sure you know exactly how it works
beforehand.

When you are ready, carry out the interview. You may be
able to write up a report on your interview which can
later be given to the other class.

2 Conrad's War
by Andrew Davies

Andrew Davies lives in Warwickshire
with his wife, two children, two cats
(Foggy and Jemima) and a silly
and soft-hearted Alsatian bitch
called Tanya.
Mostly he writes plays
for television, but he wrote *Conrad's
War* at a time when his son,
Bill, was obsessed with war,
violence, killing, tanks, blood, etc.
Bill wanted his father to write
a war book, Andrew Davies
wanted to write an anti-war book,
but they both liked funny books.
Conrad's War was the result.

* * * * * * * * * * * * *

Conrad Pike loves war and weapons. Conrad's
dad loves peace and quiet. Conrad wants a dad who
will help him build a tank. Conrad's dad wants to
be left alone to write his soppy television plays about
nurses and kissing. Then a Time Leak sucks Conrad,
his poor old dad, and their dog Towzer, back into
the Second World War. Conrad finds himself at
the controls of his own Airfix-kit Lancaster bomber,
suddenly grown huge, real and terrifying. . . .

Nuremberg, Nuremberg. They had bombed Nuremberg and now they were coming home. Conrad felt very tired. Nuremberg, he thought. A city bigger than Edinburgh, smaller than Leeds. His Gran lived in Leeds. He thought of bombers, German bombers bombing Leeds. German bombs crashing through his Gran's roof. She wouldn't know what was happening. They wouldn't be aiming for his Gran, but they might hit her all the same. Stop thinking, he said to himself, but he couldn't help it. There had to be grandmothers in Nuremberg too; Conrad wasn't stupid. Had one of his bombs fallen through someone's gran's roof? It was a bad thought, and it wouldn't go away. How did bomber pilots stop themselves from thinking bad thoughts on the slow journey home through the quiet empty sky? He reached for Towzer and sank his hand into the comforting warm fur.

"Plane coming up behind!" It was the great writer. Conrad didn't have time to do anything. A burst of cannon fire crashed into the wing of the Lancaster from the unseen Messerschmitt. Then they were alone again, left by the nightfighter to struggle and crash. Conrad checked the controls. The oil pressure was falling rapidly on the one good port engine, which was rapidly over-heating. If he didn't shut it down, he'd have a fire on his hands. He pulled the feathering toggle and leaned out to watch it splutter to a halt. They were losing height already, at the rate of five hundred feet a minute. They weren't going to get back. They had bought it.

"Get your parachute on Dad," he said. "We're going to have to jump."

"Oh no," said his Dad. "Do we have to?"

"You'll like it," said Conrad. "People pay money to do it. It's a healthy hobby Dad."

"Oh, leave off," moaned his Dad, struggling to get the straps round his fat body. "Bags I go first."

"You are first," said Conrad. "We've got to jettison the heavy stuff first, and you're the heaviest stuff here."

"But I don't speak German. Can't we wait till we get to France?"

"You'll soon pick it up," said Conrad. To his surprise, he felt quite wide awake and cheerful again. "Open the emergency door."

"Right," said his Dad. "Er, what do I do?"

"Well, you sort of jump out of the plane," said Conrad in a sarcastic voice.

"I was afraid it might be something like that," said the great writer.

"Then what?"

"You count up to five slowly and pull."

"Well, I can do that all right, I think."

"Get on and do it then," said Conrad.

"Right. Right," said his Dad. "See you later then."

"Right," said Conrad.

"Right," said his Dad. "Right, I'll just, er . . . I'll just do it now, shall I? Just sort of leap bravely out, eh?"

"YES!!!" howled the exasperated pilot.

"Right, okay then," said the writer. Conrad turned

and saw his Dad leaning gingerly out.

"I don't really much fancy the look of it down – waaaagh!" Conrad's Dad had made his first parachute jump.

The plane leapt forwards as the great weight departed, but was soon losing height again. Conrad scrabbled under the seat. One parachute. He scrabbled under the navigator's seat for a parachute for Towzer. And found a moulded grey plastic model of a parachute.

"Oh, Towzer," he said.

Towzer whined and nuzzled him. Conrad couldn't stand it. He thrust the protesting hairy legs through the straps of his own parachute and tightened them.

"You look like a bundle of old washing, Towzer," he said. Towzer looked seriously alarmed, much as he did when trapped in the kitchen with an imminent bath in store for him.

"It's not a bath, Towzer," said Conrad. "It's more a sort of a walk."

Towzer pricked his ears and wagged his tail. Before he could do anything else Conrad shoved him through the door and with a startled yelp Towzer shot out into the night.

Conrad was alone in the plane with nothing but a plastic model parachute, losing height with every second. He might never see his Dad or his Towzer again. He didn't know whether he was over the town or the country, land or water; he didn't know whether there was any chance of surviving a crash landing. He didn't know anything and it wasn't fair. The war was asking too much of him. He was only a boy.

He peered ahead. Pitch black. Nothing to be seen below. But he must be near the ground now. It would all be over soon. If he died in the crash, did that mean he'd be stuck forever in the war, an unknown casualty, and never leak back into his own world of Parkin and Creamer and the Airfix models? If he died in the crash, maybe he would leak back dead, be found in his bed stone cold with dreadful and mysterious fatal injuries. Well: somebody would be finding out soon.

He checked his instruments. Five hundred feet. He switched on the landing lights. Amazingly, they worked, and he saw the ground heaving and swaying in front of him. He had almost no control of the plane now; its strange lurches had no connection with the way he wrenched the control column to and fro. He saw sky. He saw an upside down river. He saw a forest standing on its side. He saw cloud, or was it snow? He saw sky again. He saw a road. He saw a snow-covered field, the right way up, rushing towards him at murderous speed. Height twenty feet. Ground speed a hundred miles an hour. He cut the engines and shut his eyes.

* * * * * * * * * * * * *

A. Talking about the story

1. In *Conrad's War*, Conrad gradually changes his ideas about war. At first he loves the thought of war, but by the end of the story he no longer likes it at all.

What clues in the passage tell you that Conrad is already changing his mind?

2. (a) What sort of person is Conrad's dad? How do you know?
   (b) What about Conrad himself? What clues to his character can you find in the passage?

B. Talking around the story

1. How would you feel if you had to drop bombs on an enemy city?
   How would you feel if bombs were being dropped on your city?
   If you were living during wartime, would you be prepared to join the armed forces, and kill people on the other side?
   Why do you give this answer?

2. Conrad saves Towser's life at the risk of his own. Would you do this for an animal?
   Would you do it for a person? Any person?
   Do you think that animals' lives are equal in value to people's lives? Why do you think this?

C. Activity: balloon debate

For a balloon debate, you have to imagine that about eight famous people are floating in a balloon, which is damaged and about to crash. If the balloon is to be kept airborne, all but one person must be thrown overboard. Only one person stays in the balloon — all the others must die. The passengers decide that each will make a short speech to say why he or she should be the chosen one. Then they have a secret ballot to decide whom most people think should be chosen.

A secret ballot means that each person writes down the name of the person who should win (you may not vote for yourself) on a slip of paper, folds it up and hands it to a chairman. The votes are then counted.

Work in groups of about eight.
Everyone will need a pencil and paper, and a small slip of paper for the ballot at the end. You will also need to choose someone to be chairman to run the ballot.

Everyone should choose a famous character to pretend to be. This character can be living or dead, a real person from the news or from history, or a character from fiction. Choose someone that you really admire and think should be allowed to survive the balloon disaster.

Spend a few minutes jotting down the reasons why you think your character should be saved.

When everyone in your group is ready, take it in turns to make speeches saying why *you* should stay in the balloon. (Do not read from your notes – use these only as a guide.)

After the speeches, vote in the secret ballot for the character you think most deserves to win (*not* yourself). If two or more people get the same number of votes, you should hold another ballot to decide between them.

3 Which Witch?
by Eva Ibbotson

Eva Ibbotson's parents emigrated from Russia to Germany, from there to Austria and finally to Britain. She now lives in Newcastle with her husband, occasional sons, a daughter and six Roman snails. It was partly because of a need to think up bedtime stories for her children (who are all grown up now) and partly while teaching infants, that she began to enjoy telling stories to children. She got the idea for *Which Witch?* from watching the

"Miss World Contest" on television, and thinking how much more interesting it would be if all the beautiful girls were witches.

* * * * * * * * * * * * *

Arriman the Awful of Todcaster, the Great Wizard of the North, is bored. He wants to give up wizarding and write a book. But who would take over his duties of blighting and smiting, blasting and wuthering, and keeping darkness and sorcery alive in the land? Arriman's servant, a one-eyed ogre called Lester, recommends him to go to the fortune-teller Esmeralda, and she has good news. A new wizard is on his way to Todcaster, she says, to take over Arriman's job. Arriman is delighted. He goes home and makes a three-headed monster called a Wizard Watcher to sit in his gateway watching for the new wizard. . . .

It watched in this way day after day, month after month, year after year, the Middle Head looking north over the moors, the Left-Hand Head looking west across the forest and the Right-Hand Head looking east towards the sea. Then, on the nine hundred and ninetieth day of just sitting there, the Wizard Watcher lost heart and became gloomy and annoyed.

"He cometh not from the north," said the Middle Head, as it had done every day for nine hundred and eighty-nine days.

"He cometh not from the west neither," said the Left-Hand Head.

"Nor from the east doesn't he cometh," said the Right-Hand Head. "And our feet are *freezing*."

"Our feet are blinking dropping *off*," said the Left-Hand Head.

There was a pause.

"Know what I think?" said the Middle Head. "I think the old man's been had."

"You mean there ain't going to *be* no new wizard?" said the Left-Hand Head.

The Middle Head nodded.

This time the pause was a long one.

"Don't fancy telling him," said the Right-Hand Head at last.

"Someone's got to," said the Middle Head.

So the monster turned and lumbered back to the Hall where it found Arriman in his bedroom dressing for dinner.

"Well?" he said eagerly. "What's the news?"

"The new wizard cometh not from the north," began the Middle Head patiently.

"Nor from the west he doesn't cometh," said the Left-Hand Head.

"And you can forget the east," said the Right-Hand Head, "because the new wizard doesn't cometh from there neither."

Then, speaking all together, the three heads said bravely: "We think you have been taken for a ride."

Arriman stared at them, aghast. "You can't mean it! It isn't possible!" He turned to Lester who was getting ready to trim his master's moustache. "What do you think?"

The ogre rubbed his forehead under the eye patch and looked worried. "I've never known Esmeralda make a mistake, sir. But it's been a long – "

He was interrupted by a terrible shriek from Arriman

who was peering forward into the mirror and clutching his head.

"A white hair!" yelled the magician. "A white hair in my curse curl! Oh Shades of Darkness and Perdition, this is the END!"

His shriek brought Mr Leadbetter, his secretary, hurrying into the room. Mr Leadbetter had been born with a small tail which had made him think he was a demon. This was a silly thing to think because quite a lot of people have small tails. The Duke of Wellington had one and had to have a special hole made in his saddle when he rode to battle at Waterloo. But Mr Leadbetter hadn't known about the Duke of Wellington and had wasted a lot of time trying to rob banks and so on, until he realised that crime didn't suit him and he became Arriman's secretary instead.

"Are you all right, sir?" he asked anxiously. "You seem upset."

"Upset? I'm finished! *Devastated.* Don't you know what a white hair means? It means old age, it means death. It means the end of Wizardry and Darkness and Doom at Darkington. And where is the new wizard, where, where, *where*?"

The monster sighed. "He cometh not from the north," began the Middle Head wearily.

"I know he cometh not from the north, you dolt," snapped the Great Man. "That's exactly what I'm complaining about. What am I going to *do*? I can't wait for ever."

Mr Leadbetter coughed. "Have you ever, sir, considered marriage?"

There was a sudden flash of fire from Arriman's nostrils.

"Marriage! Me marry! Are you out of your *mind*?"

"If you were to marry, sir, it would ensure the succession," said Mr Leadbetter calmly.

"What on earth are you talking about?" snapped Arriman, who was feeling thoroughly miserable and therefore cross.

"He means you could have a wizard baby, sir. Then it could take over from you. A son, you know," said Lester.

Arriman was silent. A son. For a moment he imagined the baby sitting in his pram, a dear little fellow tearing a marrow bone to shreds. Then he flinched.

"Who would I marry?" he muttered miserably.

But of course he knew. All of them knew. There is only one kind of person a wizard can marry and that is a witch.

"It wouldn't be so bad, maybe?" said the Left-Hand Head encouragingly.

"Wouldn't be so *bad*!" yelled Arriman. "Are you out of your *mind*? A great black crone with warts and blisters in unmentionable places from crashing about on her broom! You want me to sit opposite one of *those* every morning eating my cornflakes?"

"I believe witches have changed since – " began Mr Leadbetter.

But Arriman wouldn't listen. "Running along the corridors in her horrible nightgown, shrieking and flapping. Getting egg on her whiskers. Expecting her pussy cat to sleep on the bed, no doubt!"

"She might not – "

"Every time I went to the kitchen for a snack she'd be there, stirring things in her filthy pot – rubbishy frogs' tongues and newts' eyes and all that balderdash. Never a decent bit of steak in the place, I expect, once she came."

"But – "

"Cleaning her foul yellow teeth in my wash basin," raged Arriman, getting more and more hysterical. "Or worse still, *not* cleaning her foul yellow teeth in my wash basin."

"She could have her own bathroom," said the Middle Head sensibly.

But nothing could stop Arriman who stormed and ranted for another ten minutes. Then, turning suddenly very calm and pale, he said: "Very well, I see that it is my duty."

"A wise decision, sir," said his secretary.

"How shall I choose?" said Arriman. His voice was a mere thread. "It'll have to be a Todcaster witch, I suppose. Otherwise there's bound to be bad feeling. But how do we decide which witch?"

"As to that, sir," said Mr Leadbetter, "I have an idea."

* * * * * * * * * * * *

A. Talking about the story

1. What do you think Mr Leadbetter's idea might be?

2. What reasons does Arriman have for not wanting to marry a witch?

3. Arriman has three odd-looking servants. Who are they and what is odd about each one?

B. Talking around the story

1. Arriman doesn't seem to like the idea of getting old.
   Adults and children often view their birthdays differently.
   Do the adults you know welcome their birthdays?
   Do the children you know welcome theirs?
   Why is this?
   Have you ever found adults covering up about how old they were?
   Children sometimes lie about their ages too, but in what way, and why?

2. What do you think a wizard baby would look like?
   What sort of things would it be able to do?
   What would it eat?
   What problems would its parents have in bringing it up?

C. Activity: a beauty contest

Mr Leadbetter actually suggests to Arriman that the witches of Todcaster should have a contest, organised like a beauty contest, to decide which one he should marry. (It is very funny. You'll have to read the book to find out who wins.)

In groups of about six, you are going to organise a contest of this kind for witches and wizards. Choose one person to be the presenter and one to be an interviewer. The rest of the group will be contestants.

You will need paper and a pencil.

The contestants should note on their paper their names (make up good witch names!), and a little about their witchy backgrounds. They should also make brief notes about the clothes they are "wearing" for the contest. Imagine these as weird and wonderful.

Each contestant then gives these notes to the presenter and makes sure he or she understands them.

Meanwhile, the interviewer notes down some questions to ask the contestants. Usually at Beauty Contests, these are questions like "What are your hobbies?" and "What will you do if you win?" You could add some witchy ones.

When everyone is ready, the contestants should line up, and one by one, come forward to be presented.
The presenter will introduce them and describe them (and their outfit) as they arrive.
Each contestant will then be interviewed by the interviewer.

You could have a vote at the end for the best witch or wizard in your group.

Note to the teacher: The follow-up activity needs some preliminary preparation. You will find the suggested tasks in the Teacher's Book.

4 The Eighteenth Emergency
by Betsy Byars

Betsy Byars is an American and lives in West Virginia. She has been writing books for young readers ever since her own children started reading. She does her writing in the winter months, because her husband's hobby is hang-gliding and their summers are filled with working on a sailplane and driving a ten-metre trailer around to competitions. She says, "My books usually begin with something that really happened, a newspaper story or an event from my children's lives." She spends a year writing a book, but then spends another year thinking about it and improving it.

* * * * * * * * * * * *

Benjie (known as Mouse) is in trouble. He has got home from school in one piece today, but he doesn't know how much longer he can survive. At last, his friend Ezzie comes round to see him, and he rushes out to tell him his problem. . . .

He ran quickly out of the apartment and down the stairs.
Ezzie was waiting for him outside, sitting down. As soon
as he saw Mouse, Ezzie got up and said, "Hey, what
happened? Where'd you go after school?"

Mouse said, "Hammerman's after me."

Ezzie's pink mouth formed a perfect O. He didn't
say anything, but his breath came out in a long sympathetic wheeze. Finally he said, "*Marv* Hammerman?"
even though he knew there was only one Hammerman
in the world, just as there had been only one Hitler.

"Yes."

"Is after *you*?"

Mouse nodded, sunk in misery. He could see Marv
Hammerman. He came up in Mouse's mind the way
monsters do in horror movies, big and powerful, with
the same cold, unreal eyes. It was the eyes Mouse really
feared. One look from those eyes, he thought, just one
look of a certain length – about three seconds – and you
knew you were his next victim.

"What did you do?" Ezzie asked. "Or did you do
anything?"

At least, Mouse thought, Ezzie understood that. If
you were Marv Hammerman, you didn't need a reason.
He sat down on the steps and squinted up at Ezzie.
"I did something," he said.

"What?" Ezzie asked. His tongue flicked out and in
so quickly it didn't even moisten his lips. "What'd you
do? You bump into him or something?"

Mouse shook his head.

"Well, what?"

Mouse said, "You know that big chart in the upstairs hall at school?"

"What'd you say? I can't even hear you, Mouse. You're muttering." Ezzie bent closer. "Look at me. Now what did you say?"

Mouse looked up, still squinting. He said, "You know that big chart outside the history room? In the hall?"

"Chart?" Ezzie said blankly. "What chart, Mouse?"

"This chart takes up the whole wall, Ez, how could you miss it? It's a chart about early man, and it shows man's progress up from the apes, the side view of all those different kinds of prehistoric men, like Cro-Magnon man and Homo erectus. *That* chart."

"Oh, yeah, I saw it, so go on."

Mouse could see that Ezzie was eager for him to get on to the good part, the violence. He slumped. He wet his lips. He said, "Well, when I was passing this chart on my way out of history – and I don't know why I did this – I really don't. When I was passing this chart, Ez, on my way to math – " He swallowed, almost choking on his spit. "When I was passing this chart, Ez, I took my pencil and I wrote Marv Hammerman's name on the bottom of the chart and then I drew an arrow to the picture of Neanderthal man."

"What?" Ezzie cried, "*What*?" He could not seem to take it in. Mouse knew that Ezzie had been prepared to sympathise with an accident. He had almost been the victim of one of those himself. One day at school Ezzie had reached for the handle on the water fountain a second ahead of Marv Hammerman. If Ezzie hadn't glanced up just in time, seen Hammerman and said quickly, "Go ahead, I'm not thirsty," then this sagging figure on the steps might be him. "What did you do it for, Mouse?"

"I don't know."

"You crazy or something?"

"I don't know."

"Marv Hammerman!" Ezzie sighed. It was a mournful sound that seemed to have come from a culture used to sorrow. "Anybody else in the school would have been better. I would rather have the principal after me than Marv Hammerman."

"I know."

"Hammerman's big, Mouse. He's flunked a lot."

"I know," Mouse said again. There was an unwritten law that it was all right to fight anyone in your own grade. The fact that Hammerman was older and stronger made no difference. They were both in the sixth grade.

"Then what'd you do it for?" Ezzie asked.

"I don't know."

"You must want trouble," Ezzie said. "Like my grandfather. He's always provoking people. The bus driver won't even pick him up any more."

"No, I don't want trouble."

"Then, why did you – "

"I don't *know*." Then he sagged again and said, "I

didn't even know I had done it really until I'd finished. I just looked at the picture of Neanderthal man and thought of Hammerman. It does look like him, Ezzie, the sloping face and the shoulders."

"Maybe Hammerman doesn't know you did it though," Ezzie said. "Did you ever think of that? I mean, who's going to go up to Hammerman and tell him his name is on the prehistoric man chart?" Ezzie leaned forward. "Hey, Hammerman," he said, imitating

the imaginary fool, "I saw a funny thing about you on the prehistoric man chart! Now, who in their right mind is going to – "

"He was right behind me when I did it," Mouse said. "What?"

"He was right behind me," Mouse said stiffly. He could remember turning and looking into Hammerman's eyes. It was such a strange, troubling moment that Mouse was unable to think about it.

Ezzie's mouth formed the O, made the sympathetic sigh. Then he said, "And you don't even know what you did it for?"

"No."

* * * * * * * * * * * *

A. Talking about the story

1. (a) What evidence can you find in the passage that Marv Hammerman is feared by everyone in the school?
   (b) Do you think Hammerman is a good name for him? Why?
       What other names of this sort might Betsy Byars have chosen?

2. Mouse is obviously very frightened about what might happen to him. He never actually says this, but you know about it because of his actions, and the way he speaks and moves.
   Find the clues in the passage that show Mouse's fear.

B. Talking around the story

1. Marv Hammerman is a bully. Have you ever been bullied? What happened?
   Have you ever bullied anyone? Most of us have. Can you work out why you did it?
   Why do you think Hammerman is a bully?

2. Mouse does not know why he wrote Hammerman's name on the chart. Have you ever done something silly and not understood why you did it? What happened?

C. Activity: speaking without words

Prehistoric people must have gone through a stage when they had very little spoken language. They would have to communicate with signs and grunts. You are going to find out how easy or difficult this is.

Work in groups of four. Call yourselves *A*, *B*, *C* and *D*.

All the *A*'s should go to the teacher who will give them a slip of paper on which is written something which they must communicate by means of signs to the rest of the group. The group must find out what *A* is trying to say and arrange to deal with it, also using only sign language. Next, *B* should collect his message from the teacher and communicate it in the same way.

If you have time, *C* and *D* can get messages too.

Afterwards, the whole class can gather together to talk about the problems Prehistoric people must have had. What advantages are there in having a spoken language?

Other Good Reads

Anyone who likes *Which Witch?* will probably also enjoy Eva Ibbotson's *The Great Ghost Rescue** (Macmillan) about a family of ghosts who are driven out of their haunted house. There are three ghost children – Humphrey the Horrible, Wailing Winifred and George, the Screaming Skull – and their parents, the Hag and the Gliding Kilt. It's a very funny book.

So is *Grimble** by Clement Freud (Puffin). Grimble is the son of very vague parents. He arrives home one evening to find that they have gone off to Peru for a week, leaving him "Sandwiches in the oven, tea in the fridge". The story is about how he looks after himself.

For people interested in the Second World War, *What About Me?** by Gertie Everhuis (Puffin) is a gripping story set in Holland, during its occupation by the Nazis. Eleven-year-old Dirk thinks it would be exciting to become involved in the Resistance movement, but he gets more excitement (and terror) than he bargained for.

Another sort of excitement is fending for yourself, which is what Sam Gribley does in *My Side of the Mountain*** by Jean George (Puffin). He runs away from his home in New York with a penknife, a ball of string, an axe, forty dollars and some flint and steel, and lives as a "wild boy" in the Catskill Mountains.

In *Gumble's Yard *** by John Rowe Townsend (Puffin), a family of four children decide to fend for themselves when their guardian mysteriously deserts them. They set up a secret home in a derelict house, but find themselves at the centre of some suspicious goings-on.

5 Run for Your Life
by David Line

David Line has written a number of thrillers but *Run for Your Life*, a terrifying suspense story, was his first book for children. The idea for it came from his son, Philip, to whom the book is dedicated. Philip had told his father about the bullying that a foreign boy at his school was suffering. Some time later, when Philip was in bed with flu, David Line remembered these reports and began to weave a story round them for his son's entertainment. His son enjoyed it so much that David Line was encouraged to write down the nightly instalments and send them to a publisher. The book has been in print since 1966 and was made into an award-winning television serial, *Soldier and Me*.

* * * * * * * * * * * *

Soldier is a Hungarian boy who claims he has heard a group of men planning in Hungarian to murder someone. He discovers that the men are going to meet late at night in an old house, used as a language school. Soldier persuades his friend Woolcott to go there with him, and together after dark they break into the house and begin to search it. Woolcott is frightened, but Soldier is determined to carry on. Woolcott tells the story. . . .

The broad staircase was carpeted down the centre. There was a half-landing with a little room and another toilet. We rounded the bend to the first landing. Every stair creaked as you trod on it. I felt sick. Soldier's dark shape kept steadily ahead of me.

There were a couple of doors on the landing. Soldier opened them.

"Classrooms."

"Look, Soldier, what do you say if we – "

"There ought to be another room on this floor."

" – wait downstairs?"

He was away again, sniffing down the landing.

"Woolcott." The faintest murmur in the darkness.

I followed it.

There was another door, and he was inside. A sudden thick smell of stale cigar smoke.

He said, "I brought a torch. You can't see it from outside," and a pencil of light came on.

He said, "Shut the door."

I pulled it to behind me.

"Yes. This will be the room."

There were lots of books around, shelves full of books. There was a long mahogany table and leather chairs. There were thick curtains drawn across the windows.

He said, "Do you think we might switch the light on for a second?"

I practically squeaked, "For Pete's sake, no! It will show."

"We've got to have somewhere to hide here."

"Not here, Soldier! Let's wait downstairs. We don't know if they'll come here. When they come in we can see where they go and follow them – "

"No," Soldier said, "that's no good. They'd hear us coming upstairs. Probably they'll leave somebody down below to keep watch."

"Along the landing, then. We don't want to get stuck in here ... "

I heard my own voice babbling on. Soldier had already turned away and the finger of light was running along the far wall. I knew in my bones he was right – that this was the room they'd be coming in, and there was something horrible in the idea of being trapped in it, in the stale bitter cigar smoke, with thick curtains at one end, and a door at the other, and nowhere to run if we were spotted, and nobody to hear if we yelled.

He must have had an idea what was in my mind. He said, "Woolcott, if you think it would be a good idea to split up, one up here and one below – "

I said, "I don't know. What do you think?" and hoped he would think yes, so I could make a quick dash down the stairs, out through the toilet window and round the back of the house to the shelter of some welcome dripping bush. And maybe that's what I would have done, except just at that moment a door closed softly below.

There wasn't any possibility of error. It closed softly but quite firmly, and a second or two later there was a step on the stairs.

His torch had been turned on the wall, but now – I don't know why, shock maybe – it swung suddenly to the ceiling, and as the beam crossed his mouth I saw his lips moving. He seemed to be praying. The beam came down then, quickly, and swung round the room.

There was nowhere to hide. There was nowhere at all to hide. Bookshelves. Mahogany table. Curtains. I saw him going over to the curtains, and in a panic went with him, knowing it was crazy to hide behind curtains because somebody might want to open a window in the stuffy room, and then we'd be cooked, when I saw he wasn't making for the curtains.

There was a little table at the foot of the curtains. There was a china ornament on it, and under the ornament a plush tablecloth that swept to the floor.

He lifted the tablecloth and shone the torch under. There wasn't enough space there. There wasn't enough space for a cat. There were a couple of diagonal bars there to brace the legs. He flashed the torch round the room again, but it was clear there was nowhere else, so we went under the tablecloth, both of us, together.

I don't know how he organised himself. I don't know how I organised myself. I couldn't kneel, or sit, or lean, or rise. I seemed to be crouched over on my fingertips like a sprinter at the ready. And that was the position when the door opened and the light came on.

* * * * * * * * * * * *

A. Talking about the story

1. Who is the more frightened, Soldier or Woolcott? How do you know?

2. Collect all the details in the passage about the room in which they find themselves. What is it like?
   The teacher could choose one person to draw it on the blackboard according to instructions given by the rest of the class.

B. Talking around the story

1. Woolcott does not want to go on exploring the house, but Soldier ignores his objections.
   Have you ever done anything against your will because someone else urged you on? If so, what happened?
   What do you think is the best thing to do in a situation like this?

2. At the end of the passage, the boys are trapped.
   Think of some other situations in which people or animals can be trapped. Give as many examples as you can.
   Have you ever been trapped? If so, where was it?
   What does it feel like to be trapped? How do people and animals react?

C. Activity: giving clear directions

Soldier and Woolcott have been feeling their way around the old house with only a weak torch to help them. What must it be like to be blind and always in the dark?

Two people at a time are needed for this activity. One must be blindfolded and the other will be his guide. The rest of the class should watch them.

The guide must direct his partner around the room by means of spoken directions only. He must not touch him. It will be necessary to give clear directions about how to move, where to turn, what is in the way, etc. Remember to stay "Stop" at once if there is any danger.

After each pair's attempt, the class should discuss how the directions could be improved.

Note to the teacher: The follow-up activity to this passage requires a tape-recorder.

6 The White Horse Gang
by Nina Bawden

Nina Bawden has had many jobs in her life. She has worked on a farm, as a postwoman and as a town planner. Now she writes books for both adults and children. Nina has no use for children's books that show that adults are always kind, helpful and wise, but much prefers to produce real-life situations in her books in which adults are often "half-way to being villains". She is married and has two sons and a daughter.

* * * * * * * * * * * *

Sam Peach, his cousin Rose and their scruffy friend Abe Tanner are miserable because they need money but cannot think of any way to raise it. Rose is staying with Sam's family while her parents are in America but she is so homesick that she wants to raise the money for the air-fare to go and see them. While Sam and Abe are on their way to school one afternoon, they meet Percy Mountjoy, a spoilt little mummy's darling who isn't allowed to play with nasty, rough boys. . . .

Full of melancholy, they collected the best of the conkers and stuffed their pockets. The school bell began to clang across the field, and, sighing, they made their slow way towards another long afternoon's boredom. At the edge of the field, Percy Mountjoy appeared from behind a tree.

"Hullo, Sam," he said.

Sam was too dispirited to be rude to him. "Lo," he said weakly.

"You been collecting conkers?" Percy asked. He was wearing grey linen shorts buttoning on to a blue shirt, his pale hair was licked down dark with water and fastened with – of all things! – a girl's tortoise-shell hair slide. Abe and Sam looked at him with distaste.

"How old are you?" Abe asked.

"Seven, going on eight. Would you like to see my double one?" He held out a beautiful nut with the burr split neatly open and showing the soft white inside and the two perfect, glossy nuts. "You can have it if you like," he said. Both boys looked at the nut enviously, but made no move to take it.

"Don't you want it?" Percy said in a disappointed voice. He put it back in his pocket. "I'm going to the circus on Monday," he said importantly. "Are you going to the circus, Sam?"

"I expect so." A thought struck him. "Why haven't you gone back to school?"

"I'm not going back for another week. I've had a nasty cold."

Abe and Sam looked at each other. "Only babies stay at home because they've got colds," Sam said.

Percy's pale cheeks went pink. "I'm not a baby. Can I play with you after tea?"

They hesitated. Percy was innocent and silly as a baby duck and they were too despondent, at this moment, to be deliberately unkind to him. But the decision was taken out of their hands.

"Percy!" Mrs Mountjoy was leaning out of the window of her house. "PERCY! Come here this minute!"

Percy glanced over his shoulder at his mother and turned back to the boys. "*Can* I?" he pleaded urgently.

"Your Mam wants you jus' now," Abe said and, taking Percy by the shoulders, gave him a little push towards the road. This gesture was misunderstood by Mrs Mountjoy, who shouted in a paroxysm of rage that Abe was to let her Percy go, now, this very minute! "Don't you dare put your hands on him," she screamed. "You dreadful, vulgar boy!"

Abe whipped his hands back as if he had been stung. Percy hurried across the road without looking and only just missed being knocked down by an old man on a bicycle. This near-accident produced a fresh torrent of abuse from Mrs Mountjoy who threatened Abe with the police, with his Headmaster, and with her own revenge, if only she could get her hands on *him*.

"Come away," Sam urged, as Abe stood staring at his enemy and going first, red, then white.

But Abe did not move until Mrs Mountjoy vacated

the window and appeared at her front door. She drew
Percy inside the house and shut the door with an angry
slam. Abe drew a long, quivering sigh and followed Sam
silently, back to school. He did not speak until they
were at the door of the classroom. Then he caught
Sam's sleeve and held him back. "I got an idea," he
whispered. "It's a good idea, 'cause it'll do two things –
get our own back and make some money. Want to hear?"

Sam nodded and Abe put his mouth to his ear. "We
c'n kidnap Percy Mountjoy," he said.

* * * * * * * * * * * *

A. Talking about the story

1. Scan the passage for information about the way Mrs Mountjoy is bringing up her son, Percy.
   (a) What sort of things is she strict about?
   (b) How does she like him to dress?
   (c) Find two ways in which she tries to protect him from the outside world.

2. Abe and Percy speak very differently from each other.
   (a) Find some of the things they say in the passage which show the differences in the way they speak.
   (b) Try saying some of these speeches in voices suitable for Abe and Percy. Why do you think the voices you chose are suitable ones?

B. Talking around the story

1. Sam, Rose and Abe *do* kidnap Percy, with disastrous results.
   How easy do you think it would be to kidnap another child?
   How would you go about it, and what would be the difficulties?
   Do you know of any real-life kidnappings? Tell the class about any you know of.

2. "I've had a nasty cold," says Percy. Where do you think he picked up this soppy expression?

Do any adults you know use any soppy, funny, or odd expressions?

What are they?

Do you ever pick up expressions from other people? What are they?

C. Activity: taped messages

Since telephone answering machines became popular, there are many occasions when you have to communicate messages quickly and clearly on to a tape.

Different members of the class can try one of these tasks each.

They should speak their message into the tape-recorder as though it were a telephone answering machine.

Before they begin, the whole class should discuss what information must be given each time.

After each message is recorded, it can be played back and you can discuss how successful it is and whether it could be improved.

(a) A message to a doctor, asking him to visit a sick child.
(b) A message to a hotel to reserve a room.
(c) A message arranging to meet a business friend for lunch.
(d) A message asking for an appointment with a head-teacher, to discuss your child's progress at school.

7 The Ogre Downstairs
by Diana Wynne Jones

Diana Wynne Jones has a labrador with a soppy nature
and strong opinions who bosses her around all the time.
He sits in her study while she is writing — or he is upside
down snoring — and when she has finished a book, he
always manages to lie on it. Everything she has written
so far has been fantasy, and a great deal of it comic; she
likes to provide exciting and amusing reading for children.
In her books, magic is first an extra problem for her
characters, and then — if they can master it — a way of
solving their difficulties.

After their father's death, Johnny, Caspar and their little sister, Gwinny, have got used to having their mother to themselves. So when she marries again, they do not take kindly to their new stepfather, who is rather bad-tempered and shouts a lot. They nickname him "the Ogre". To make things worse, the Ogre brings his own two sons to live with them. They are called Douglas and Malcolm, and they seem a snobbish, unfriendly pair.

One evening, the Ogre unexpectedly brings home two enormous unusual-looking chemistry-sets, and gives one to Johnny and one to Malcolm. But before Johnny can settle down to make disgusting smells with his set, the order comes that he and Caspar must tidy their bedroom – and that the Ogre will be up soon to inspect it. . . .

This threat was enough to cause Johnny and Caspar a little energetic work. By the time the Ogre's heavy feet were heard on the stairs, Caspar had piled books, papers and records in a sort of heap by the wall, and Johnny had pushed most of the construction-kits under his bed and the cupboard, so that, apart from the chemistry-set, the floor was almost clear.

The Ogre stood in the doorway with his hands in his pockets and his pipe in his mouth and looked round the room with distaste. "You do like to live in squalor, don't you?" he said. "I suppose all those toffee-bars *are* an essential part of your diet? O.K. I'll report a clear floor. How are you getting on with that chemistry-set?"

"I like it," Johnny said, with a polite smile. "But I've been too busy clearing up to use it yet."

The Ogre's heavy eyebrows went up, and he looked rather pointedly round the room. "I'll leave you to it, then," he said. A thought struck him. "I suppose I ought in fairness to make a surprise inspection over the way," he said. They watched him turn and walk across the landing. They saw him open the door to Malcolm's and Douglas's room. They waited hopefully. It would be wonderful if, for once, it was those two who got into trouble.

Nothing happened, however, except for a surprisingly strong stench, which swept across the landing and made Caspar cough. Malcolm's voice followed it. "This chemistry-set is positively brilliant, Father! Look at this."

"Having fun, are you?" said the Ogre, and he shut the door rather hastily and went downstairs.

"Pooh!" said Caspar.

"I just like that!" said Johnny. "If it had been us making a smell like that, we wouldn't half have got it! All right then. Watch me after supper. I'll make the worst stink you ever smelt, and if he says anything, I'll say, what about Malcolm?"

Johnny was as good as his word. After supper, he set to work in the middle of the carpet, mixing all the strongest and likeliest-looking things from the various tubes and phials and heating them with the spirit-lamp to see what happened. When he found a good smell, he poured it carefully into a toothmug and mixed another. The savour of the room went through rotten cabbage, elderly egg, mouldy melon, gasworks and bad breath; blue smoke hung about in it. Caspar, who was lying on his bed doing History homework, coughed considerably, but he bore it in a good cause.

When Gwinny came in instead of going to bed, she was exquisitely disgusted. She sat beside Johnny in her pink nightdress, wriggling her bare toes and pretending to smoke one of the Ogre's pipes that she had stolen. "Eeugh!" she said, and peered at Johnny's flushed face through the gathering smoke. "We look like a witches' convent. Caspar looks like a devil looming through the smoke."

"Coven," said Caspar. "Devil yourself."

Giggling, Gwinny stuck her spiky hair out round her head and carefully tapped some of the ash out of the pipe into the toothmug. The mixture fizzed a little. "Do you think it'll explode now?" she asked hopefully.

"Shouldn't think so," said Johnny. "Move, or you'll get burnt."

"Is it smelly enough?" asked Gwinny.

"I still haven't found the one Malcolm got," admitted Johnny.

"Try a dead fish or so. That should do it," Caspar suggested. Gwinny squealed with laughter.

"*Gwinny!*" boomed the voice of the Ogre. "*Are you in bed?*"

Gwinny dropped the pipe, jumped up and fled. In her

hurry, she knocked the toothmug flying and Johnny was too late to save it. Half the mixture spilt on the carpet. The rest splashed muddily on Gwinny's legs and nightdress. Gwinny squealed again as she raced for the door. "It's *cold*!" But she dared not stop to apologise. She continued racing, up the next stairs and into her little room on the top floor. She left behind her the most appalling smell. It was worlds worse than the one Malcolm had produced. It was so horrible that it awed them. They were staring at one another in silence, when Gwinny began to scream.

"Caspar! Johnny! Caspar! Oh, come *quickly*!"

Caspar and Johnny pelted up to Gwinny's room regardless of noise. Johnny thought she was on fire, Caspar that she was being eaten away by acids. They burst into the room and stood staring. Gwinny did not seem to be there. Her lamp was lit, her bed was empty, her window shut, and her doll's house and all her other things arranged around as usual, but they could not see Gwinny.

"She's gone," said Caspar helplessly.

"No I haven't," said Gwinny, her voice quivering rather. "I'm up here." Both their heads turned upwards. Gwinny appeared to be hanging from the ceiling. Her shoulders were lodged in the corner where the roof stopped sloping and turned into flat ceiling, her bony legs were dangling straight down beneath her, and her hands were nervously clasped in front of her. She looked a bit like a puppet. "And I can't come down," she added.

"However did you get up?" demanded Johnny.

"I sort of floated," said Gwinny. "I went all light after that stuff splashed on me, and while I was getting into bed I got so light that I just went straight up and stayed here."

"Lordy!" said Johnny.

* * * * * * * * * * * *

A. Talking about the story

1. (a) What do you think caused Gwinny to fly?
   (b) How do you think the others will manage to get her down?

2. (a) What is an ogre?
   (b) What details in the passage suggest to you that the Ogre is well-named?

B. Talking around the story

1. Have you ever wished you could fly?
   Have you ever dreamt about flying? If so, how do you go about flying in your dreams?
   Have you ever flown in an aeroplane? If so, what was it like?
   What advantages and disadvantages would there be in being able to fly?

2. The chemistry-set in *The Ogre Downstairs* turns out to be magic, and Johnny makes other potions which have strange effects. One of these potions makes everyday objects come to life. The Ogre's pipe comes to life and acts like a little squirrel, and the bits of construction kit on the floor act like wriggly worms.
   If you could bring an everyday object to life, what would you choose? How do you think it would act?

C. Activity: hat talks

Divide into groups of about six and choose a group leader. The group should decide on ten topics which will be the subjects of short, unprepared talks. You could choose topics like Magic, Flying, My Family, Tidying my Room or any other topics you like.

The leader then writes these topics on slips of paper, folds them and puts them into a container of some sort.

The group members take it in turns to pull a topic out of the container. Whatever it is, that person must speak for one minute exactly on that subject. One person in the group should be the official time-keeper.

Other Good Reads

Mike and Me** by David Line (Puffin) also features the heroes of *Run for Your Life*. It has a couple of slow chapters early on, but a thrilling adventure develops.

Another thriller is *The Boy Who Knew Too Much** by Roderic Jeffries (Puffin). Roger Brent sneaks into a factory building for a dare, and finds himself terrifyingly involved in a mysterious crime.

For humour mixed with adventure, *The Size Spies** by Jan Needle (Fontana) is a good read. After an accident with a crazy invention, Cynthia and George's parents are shrunk to the size of goldfish. The children must contact the Government for help, while trying to prevent the shrinking machine from falling into the hands of crooks, who want to use it to rule the world!

Adventure and sport are mixed together in Michael Hardcastle's series of football books, which trace the career of a boy called Mark Fox from his school team to the world of professional football. The first two books are *The First Goal** and *Breakaway** (Armada).

If you enjoyed the fantasy of *The Ogre Downstairs*, you'll probably love *Half Magic**** by Edward Eager (Puffin). It's about a family of children who find a magic coin that can make wishes come true. But, since the coin is only *half* magic, they only get half of each wish!

Finally, we recommend a very funny little book of short stories, *Elephants Don't Sit on Cars** by David Henry Wilson (Piccolo). Jeremy Jones is a naughty little boy who is always getting into trouble. In the first story he tells his mother that there's an elephant sitting on Daddy's car and, of course, she doesn't believe him. . . .

8 Space Hostages
by Nicholas Fisk

Nicholas Fisk wrote his first book when he was nine. It was about a baby fox and was very sentimental. He first earned money for writing when he was sixteen. Nowadays he concentrates mainly on writing "science fiction" books for young people. He likes to pick on a possibility — something extraordinary — and then fit it into the ordinary world, showing how ordinary people behave in a strange situation. He likes writing for young people because they seem to understand how fast the world is changing, whereas most older people don't.

* * * * * * * * * * * *

A mysterious space-ship has landed in the village of Little Mowlesbury. The man in control of it, a Flight Lieutenant, says that the ship belongs to the Government and offers to take some of the local children aboard to show them around. Three girls and five boys go up in the lift with him, then. . . .

"Back in half a minute for the next . . . " said the Flight Lieutenant from inside the lift. Then there was a metallic click as if he had disconnected some vital plug. Then the whirring whine as the lift ascended, a little glimmer of light rising up into the belly of the ship. Then the closing of the underbelly doors so that one could no longer see that there had been a lift at all. Then another click, and the voice of the Flight Lieutenant, speaking through a louder, harsher amplifier and in a louder, harsher tone:

"CLEAR THE GROUND. Get away from the ship. Clear the ground. GET WELL AWAY. CLEAR THE GROUND."

Mrs Mott screamed first. There were more screams, then a roar of voices and a surging of the crowd under the ship. The four guns were raised, but the Flight Lieutenant's voice said, "None of that!" and the guns wavered and were brought down.

"He must have TV in there," began Jim Knowles.

"YOU HAVE TEN SECONDS," said the great metal voice, flatly. "NINE ... EIGHT ... SEVEN YOU'D BETTER MOVE AND MOVE FAST! – SIX – CLEAR THE GROUND, FIVE ..."

Some people moved and one or two ran.

"FOUR ... THREE ... TWO ... " A whole crowd ran for the edge of the meadow. "ONE! ALL RIGHT. I TOLD YOU TO MOVE ... "

There was a thunderous bellow from the black shape above them – a sound so loud that people screamed from the pain of it and fell to the ground, their hands over their ears. The bellowing stopped. Slowly the figures rose and walked, dazed. The voice spoke again.

"YOU HAVE A MATTER OF SECONDS. HELP EACH OTHER OFF THE GROUND. CLEAR THE GROUND. I AM GOING TO TAKE OFF."

The vicar looked up at the glinting metallic blackness, and whispered, "But you said you couldn't! You lied!" Next to him old Durden fell down and lay gasping.

"CLEAR THE GROUND. CLEAR THE GROUND. YOU PEOPLE THERE AROUND THE OLD MAN LIFT HIM UP AND GET HIM AWAY. DO IT NOW. CLEAR THE GROUND. I AM GOING TO TAKE OFF."

"Ashley!" screamed Mrs Mott. She ran to one of the great legs of the ship and hit it with her fists.

"CLEAR THE GROUND. GET THAT WOMAN AWAY. YOU TWO MEN, TAKE THAT WOMAN AWAY. CLEAR THE GROUND, YOU HAVE VERY LITTLE TIME."

A new noise, a thin electronic scream, came from the ship. The scream rose higher and higher and settled to a single steady note. "THAT'S RIGHT, CLEAR THE GROUND. THAT'S GOOD. NOW KEEP WALK-ING. WALK AWAY. GET WELL CLEAR. KEEP WALKING. GET WELL CLEAR. YOU HAVE ONLY SECONDS LEFT!"

Women were crying and stumbling. Knowles fired six shots from his rifle in quick succession. You could see the spark and glitter where the bullets hit the ship. The Flight Lieutenant's voice, suddenly quiet and tired, said, "Don't be a silly man." Then the voice came back, not so loud.

"Now listen. Your children are coming with me. As long as I last. They will find a way, somewhere, somehow. Away from this world." The voice faltered.

"He's ill," whispered the Vicar.

"He's mad," said Mr Knowles.

Almost as if he had heard him, the Flight Lieutenant said, "Perhaps you think I am mad. I think you are mad. Yes, all of you. The news – surely you must realise by now what is going to happen. War, destruction, everywhere. The whole world. And you do nothing, nothing. Someone must do . . ." They could hear him coughing.

Then, "Hostages to fortune, that's the sort of nonsense you understand. Your children are hostages to fortune. They can start again when you lot have destroyed yourself and your world. You should thank me. You should . . ."

Silence for a few seconds. Then the voice spoke for the last time:

"GET CLEAR. TURN YOUR HEADS. DO NOT WATCH. LIE DOWN. I AM GOING TO TAKE OFF NOW. I AM GOING TO TAKE OFF NOW. COVER YOUR HEADS AND GUARD YOUR EYES. THE CHILDREN ARE ... "

There was the noise of an express train, then twenty express trains, then a tearing shriek of blasting jets. The great craft seemed bathed in fire. It rose slowly, slowly, and the legs entered the body. The fury of the noise increased. The people clutched their heads. Their mouths were O's, but their screaming could not be heard above the huge outcry of the ship. It rose, still slowly, then faster. Then much faster.

People raised their heads and looked. They saw a dwindling point of fire in the sky, heard the rumbling express train noise booming and re-echoing among their familiar little hills.

It was gone.

A. Talking about the story

1. Look at the kind of print used for the words spoken by the Flight Lieutenant. Some of his words are printed in capital letters and others are not.
   (a) Find all the speeches he makes which are not in capital letters.
   (b) Why do you think some of his speeches are in capitals and some aren't? What is the difference in the way he is speaking in each case?

2. (a) The Flight Lieutenant is very ill. In fact, he is going to die soon. What signs of this are there in the passage?
   (b) When he dies, the children are all alone in the space-ship. What do you think will happen to them?

B. Talking around the story

1. The Flight Lieutenant says that the children are now hostages. What is a hostage?
   Why has the Flight Lieutenant taken the children hostage?
   Why are hostages usually taken?
   Do you know of any occasions in real life when hostages have been taken? Tell the class about them.

2. Once the Flight Lieutenant dies, the children are left to cope on their own. Have you ever had to cope in a difficult situation with no adults around to help?

Think of as many situations as you can, from the news, from history or from fiction, where children have had to cope on their own. Discuss how successful they were.

C. Activity: group discussion

Work in groups of six to eight. Each group should have a leader to organise the discussion and take notes so that he or she can report back.
You are going to discuss "Space Exploration: For or Against".

The Americans, Russians and many other nations spend an enormous amount of money on research into vehicles that can go into space and explore it. Why do you think they place such value on space exploration?

"All opportunities for exploring space should be eagerly seized, no matter what the cost." Discuss this statement, and note all the points for and against it.

At the end of your discussion, take a vote for or against "Space Exploration".

The group leaders can then report back to the class on their group's decisions, and the main reasons for reaching these decisions.

Note to the teacher: The follow-up activity to this passage requires a tape-recorder.

9 Me and My Million
by Clive King

Clive King's most famous book is *Stig of the Dump*, which has been televised as a serial. He was born in Richmond, Surrey, in 1924 and his first name is David. While he was at Cambridge University, the Second World War broke out, and Clive left his studies to serve in the Royal Naval Volunteer Reserve. Later he worked for the British Council and travelled widely overseas.

* * * * * * * * * * * *

Ringo doesn't think much of school – he can't read and he gets numbers mixed up. But he's very pleased when his big brother Elvis asks him to help do a robbery! Elvis and his friend Shane are planning to steal a picture worth a million pounds. They ask Ringo to wait near the art gallery and take the stolen picture in a laundry bag to Tottenham Hale, far across London. He has to catch two buses to get there, then go to a launderette and hand over the bag to a blonde girl called Marilyn.

When the night of the robbery comes, Ringo collects the laundry bag, catches the first bus, then changes to the second. . . .

I hadn't had time to warm up on the other bus but I was getting quite cosy now with the warm air blowing on my feet. And now I could think about what I'd got with me.

I thought of the picture, the way I'd seen it hanging on the wall in the old house. I looked at the bag and gave it a squeeze. There didn't seem to be room for all that knobbly gold frame in that wash bag. How much would a picture like that weigh? The bag didn't seem all that heavy.

Maybe it *was* just a load of old socks.

I squeezed it again. There was something hard in there. I can tell you I wanted to unwrap the bundle of sheets and have a good look. But the bus was beginning to fill up.

I looked out of the bus window into the dark. Outside there was this big castle, with all towers and that. If I had a million pounds – if it *was* a million pounds that I'd got – I could buy myself a castle. I wondered what sort of castle it was, out there in that bit of London.

"Anyone for Holloway jail?" calls the conductor. Well, perhaps I'd buy another castle somewhere. That place was for the bad birds.

We came to the road where there's the two big railway stations. Now I was rich I could get on any train I liked, go anywhere I liked. Go to the sea and get on a boat and sail away. Except I'd only got two pee in my pocket, until I could get rid of that picture.

If it *was* the picture.

We came to the bit where there's all buildings with big words in bright lights in front of them. I knew they were the theatres where you could go and see the rock stars and the actors and actresses. They were the ones with the money. But how many of *them* had a million-pound picture like me? I could buy a pop group, be their manager!

If it *was* a million-pound picture that I had.

The conductor called out, "Piccadilly!" People got out to look at all the letters and pictures in bright lights. We went on and there were glass windows with big model jet planes in them. That was where you went to buy your air ticket to America or Australia. If I could get there, maybe I could sell this old picture, and no questions asked. But I only had this two pee.

The bus went past big glass windows with big shiny cars in them. I'd have a Jag and a Rolls to begin with. But I had to find this launderette first.

Shops selling pictures! Maybe they'd buy mine. But they were all shut. And anyway, you don't just take the loot into any old shop, do you?

This bus ride seemed to go on for ever. Ordinary houses both sides of the road. The conductor calls out, "Stamford Bridge!" That's the football ground, but nobody gets off this time of night. You know what? – I could buy a whole football team! Not *Chelsea* though.

Now there was a big bridge over water. Elvis had said something about water-works, the River Lea, near the end of the run. I stopped worrying.

I asked the conductor if we were near the end of the run. "Next stop," he said. The bus was nearly empty.

We came to the stop and the conductor called out, "All change!" I picked up the bag and got out of the warm bus into the cold street.

I looked around. Elvis had said all I had to do was get to the end of the run and I'd find a launderette. And there it was, the launderette, rows of white machines inside a steamy window. I'd done it.

I pushed open the glass door. It was warmer than the bus inside. A few women sitting around smoking, waiting for their wash to finish. Some kids fooling around, listening to a transistor. Where was this Marilyn bird who was supposed to be waiting for me?

The black lady who seemed to be running the place came up to me. "Can I help you, love?" she says.

"I got this wash, for Marilyn," I said.

"Don't know no Marilyn, darling," she says. "Closing in half an hour. Last wash going in now."

And she grabs the bag from me, opens the front of a big machine, and begins to stuff handfuls of old socks and shirts into it. And there's the big square thing all wrapped up in sheets going in too!

I had to give her a good hard shove out of the way and grab it all back again. You can't put a million-pound picture through the wash, can you? The colours might run or something.

"All right love, don't have to shove!" says the launder-ette lady. "Some folks don't want to be helped," she

says to the other women.

"I got no money," I said. "Not till this Marilyn comes. She's got blonde hair, jeans."

"Plenty like that, dearie," says the lady, moving off. "Anyone know a Marilyn?" she asks the other women.

They shook their heads and their cigarettes waggled. "There's a Marion something, comes here," says one. "Black hair though, always wears them long skirts."

I was beginning to wonder if it was the right place. "Is there another launderette in Tottenham Hale?" I asked.

"Tottenham Hale?" they said back at me stupidly, and waggled their fags again. "Don't know no Tottenham Hale neither," says one of them.

There was an old man sitting quietly in a corner doing one of these crossword puzzles. They're like the pools,

I think, only there's not much money in them. He says, "Tottenham Hale? That's the other side of London. Right up in E four. Must be ten miles away."

"Where's this then?" I asked.

"This is Putney, ducks," says the black woman.

Putney! What was the use of Putney? That nit Elvis, with his number forty-ones and his fag packets!

"My brother said the forty-one bus goes to Tottenham Hale," I said.

"I don't know about no forty-one bus," says one of the women.

"But I just got *off* one, in the street there!" I said.

"Ah, that'd be a fourteen, wouldn't it?" says another. "Not the same, is it?"

They looked at each other and one of them said, "Don't teach them a thing at school nowadays, do they?"

Silly lot of old pigeons! I got that feeling like I wanted to kick in the glass fronts of all their silly washing machines.

"Well, how do I get back home then?" I shouted at them. "I've got no money!"

"We've heard that story and all," says a woman.

"It's what all the old drunks say, ain't it?" says another.

"Kids too, now. They're picking it up," says another.

Well, I'd done it myself, for a lark. But now I *needed* it!

The old man in the corner says, "There's a police station up the street, son. They'll see you home if you're really lost."

And just then the kids with the transistor tuned in to the news and I heard the announcer say:

" ... North London, and news just come in of a big art robbery. In a lightning smash and grab raid on the public gallery at Kenwood House, thieves got away with one of the nation's most valuable pictures. They abandoned the gold frame in the nearby woods, but there's no trace of the thieves or the picture. The value of the painting – one and a half million pounds!"

My legs went weak and I sat down on the bench by the drying machines. It was true then! Up to now it had been like a game, something between me and Elvis and Shane. But now it was on the news, and all the world knew about it. And it had gone up to a million and a half already!

* * * * * * * * * * * * *

A. Talking about the story

1. All through the journey, Ringo daydreams of the things he could buy. What does he want to buy and do with a million pounds?

2. Although he did not mean to go there, Ringo finds himself in Putney. How has this mistake happened?

B. Talking around the story

1. Where do the names Elvis and Ringo come from? Would you like a name of this sort?

What would be the advantages and disadvantages?
What do you think of the name you have got?
Why did your parents choose it for you?

2. What would you buy with a million pounds?

C. Activity: newscasting

Your teacher will ask someone to read aloud the news broadcast at the end of the passage in the way that a real newscaster would speak it.

You are now going to put together a news bulletin on tape. Work in pairs. You will need a pencil and paper.
Each pair should choose an item of real news to report. It could be recent international or national news, local news from your area, or something interesting that has happened recently at school.

When you have chosen your news item, tell your teacher what it is, so that she can make sure that everyone has chosen something different.

Discuss the topic and make notes about it. Invent a good headline with which to begin your item.

Decide which of you is to be the newscaster. If you are the newscaster, you should practise how you will announce the news. Your partner should listen and help you to improve it.

When your teacher calls the class together you can discuss in which order the items should be put on the tape.

10 Fish
by Alison Morgan

Alison Morgan lives in Wales. She is married with two sons, and once was a secondary school teacher. Now she does lots of voluntary activities, mainly for young people. She has written pantomimes and religious plays which have been performed in the village where she lives.

Another book of hers, *At Willie Tucker's Place*, follows the adventures of Jimmy Price's younger brother, who is mad on the army.

* * * * * * * * * * * *

James Barnes, nicknamed Fish, has just moved to a Welsh farming village, where he is still very much an outsider. He also has problems with his strict and unpleasant father. One day, Fish and another boy, Jimmy Price, are walking home from a football game. Jimmy Price tells the story. . . .

We crossed the main road and were just starting up our lane when something caught Fish's eye.

"Look," he said, "a dog." I stepped back and glanced up the main road. A leggy mongrelly sort of animal was

72

bounding down the road towards us, but when it got about six feet away it stopped and cringed, wagging its tail and looking guilty all at the same time, like sheepdogs often do when they can't be sure whether you are going to hit them or pat them. Only this wasn't a sheepdog, or at least most of it wasn't. It was some kind of hairy long-legged terrier, very dirty and very thin.

"I've never seen that dog before," I said. "It doesn't live around here."

Fish held out his fingers. "Here, boy," he said. "Come on then." The animal edged itself forward on its tummy, its tongue going in and out, and its tail sweeping across the tarmac, but cautious. Its ears kept flickering up and down – up for anxiety, down flat for love and affection. I went to stroke it, and it flew up the road.

"You've frightened it," said Fish.

"Not for long," I answered, and the dog soon came back, squirming round us in a circle, keeping just out of reach. Fish stayed crouched down, and after a while

the dog came close enough to sniff at his elbow. Fish slowly put out his other hand and after letting the dog sniff his fingers he ran them gently up the side of its nose. Suddenly the dog went wild with excitement. It threw itself all over Fish, licking his face, scratching his precious anorak with its dirty paws, pressing its muddy body against him.

Fish, surprisingly, didn't seem to mind. He made a few feeble efforts to keep the dog down, but he loved it really.

"Down, dog," he said, and it rolled over on its back, then up again. I noticed it was a bitch, and said so.

"Is he?" said Fish.

"She," I said.

"Is she?" he asked. "How do you know?"

It's funny the things Fish doesn't know. I suppose it comes of spending most of his life in a town. At least, I wasn't sure where he had lived, because according to Fish he had lived in a lot of places, but his family had only been at the Ferns for three months, and they weren't ordinary country people like the rest of us, and yet they weren't exactly towny either. They were the kind of people who did not seem to belong anywhere.

I told Fish how I knew she was a bitch, and he seemed quite interested, but then his mind went on to the next thing.

"Do you think she belongs to anyone?" he said.

"She must belong to *somebody*," I said.

"Perhaps she's just a stray," said Fish. He hugged her

tight. I went to stroke her, but she still seemed a bit nervous of me, and backed away.

"She likes me best," said Fish.

"She's made you very dirty," I retorted. "What will your dad say now?"

"Oh, I'll say one of the boys rolled me in the ditch," said Fish. "That will explain how it got tore, too."

I thought that was a bit mean, but Fish was like that. You could never trust him. He'd think up any kind of story rather than take the blame for something himself.

Fish had been sitting quiet, hugging the dog. "I'm going to keep her," he said. He sounded frightened, yet defiant.

"You can't," I said. "Somebody will claim her."

"Who?" said Fish.

"Whoever she belongs to."

"I don't think her owner wants her any more. I think she's just been abandoned."

"How do you mean, abandoned?" Of course you have to drown puppies just like kittens if nobody wants them, but I didn't see how you could just turn out a half-grown dog like this one. It would come back again, anyway. All the same, if ever I saw an unwanted-looking dog, this was it. Except that Fish wanted it, wanted it very badly.

"She's getting big enough to need a licence," said Fish. I did not know much about that, because none of our dogs need licences, being working sheepdogs, but this one looked kind of half-dog, half-puppy age, daft and fun like a puppy, but almost as big as a full-grown dog.

"There's lots of dogs abandoned when they get old enough to need a licence," Fish went on. "It's easy, if you're moving house. You just leave the dog behind."

"How do you know?" I asked. "I bet you're just making it up because you want to keep her."

"It's true, anyway," said Fish. "I know because – I just know."

* * * * *

But Fish still has to convince his dad to let him keep the dog. The two boys approach his home, and Mr Barnes is waiting. . . .

"Is that you, James?" called Mr Barnes, harshly. Then he saw I was there, too. "Why, it's Jimmy Price, isn't it?" he went on, in quite a different tone of voice. "My word, you're growing into a fine boy. Seeing you in the dark there I thought you were your father. Hey James, when are we going to see you grow into a fine boy like Jimmy?" He made it sound as though it were all Fish's fault that he was not as tall as me.

I don't know any grown-up that I disliked talking to as much as Mr Barnes. He always spoke to me as though I were an important grown-up whom he particularly wanted to impress, like Mr Thomas. I was sure he couldn't really be thinking of me in that way, so I knew it was just a sham, but what I could not understand was

what he was getting at. I think really he was getting at
Fish.

"Please, Dad," said Fish.

"Well, what is it *now*?" said Mr Barnes, as though it
were the sixtieth time Fish had asked him for something,
when in fact it was the only thing he had said. "Always
whining for something, this boy is. You won't catch
Jimmy Price whining for things, you may be sure of that."

"Please Dad, I've got this dog."

"*You've* got a dog? Don't be ridiculous."

"It *is* mine. It's a stray, and ... "

"You brought it here."

"Yes. Because ... "

"You found a dirty, filthy, stray dog from goodness
knows where, and you brought it here. Why, may I
ask?" It wasn't the kind of question Fish was meant
to answer. "Why you, and not Jimmy? I'll tell you,
Jimmy has more sense than to pick up every disease-
ridden thieving stray animal that he finds and take it
into his nice clean house."

"Mr Thomas Tygwyn gave it me." Give Fish credit,
he could tell a lie as though it were the truest, most
matter-of-fact thing in the world. "He found it hanging
around the yard, and he's ringing the police to ask
them if they can find the owner. He asked me if I'd
look after it for him, seeing as we haven't got a dog.
He was afraid it would fight with his dogs if he put it
in the shed with them."

It came over ever so natural. Fish sounded whining,

but then he always sounded like that when he was talking to his father.

I began to move on up the hill. I hadn't actually said anything about the dog, but I had listened to Fish's tale without ever openly contradicting him, so I thought I'd done my share.

"You off home, Jimmy Price?" said Mr Barnes. "I wish you could spare the time some day to teach my son to speak the truth. You just can't believe a word he says." He turned to Fish. "Be off indoors, you," he said. "I'll soon see this creature is sent about his business."

* * * * * * * * * * * *

A. Talking about the story

1. Do you agree with Fish that the dog has been abandoned? Or do you agree with Jimmy, the narrator, that she probably still belongs to somebody? Give evidence from the passage to support your opinion.

2. Why do you think that owning this dog is so important to Fish? Which parts of the passage make you think this?

3. What do you notice about the way Mr Barnes addresses Jimmy Price, compared with the way he talks to his own son, James (Fish)? Why do you think he speaks to Jimmy Price in the way he does?

B. Talking around the story

1. Have you ever wanted to have a pet that you were not allowed to have? What were the reasons that you could not have it?

2. Fish tells a lot of lies. Why do you think this is?
   Most children tell lies now and then. How do people feel when they are telling lies? Is it pleasant?
   Why should people try to tell the truth whenever they can?
   Are there ever occasions when it is better to lie than to tell the truth?

C. Activity: speaking to different sorts of people

The way Mr Barnes varies his manner of speech when talking to the two boys is rather unpleasant. But we all have to vary the way we speak when talking to different sorts of people. For instance, you wouldn't talk in the same way to your best friend and to the Prime Minister.

This activity is designed to show how we vary the way we speak. Two people are needed to act out an example to the class. They should call themselves *A* and *B*.

A should think of an occasion when he was in trouble at school or at home. He then tells *B* about it, talking as he would to a very good friend of his own age. He should recount it as clearly as possible, saying what happened and how he thought about it at the time.

B should listen carefully and ask questions when necessary to get the story really clear in his mind.

Then *A* pretends to be a headteacher, sitting behind a desk looking important. *B* tells the same story, but this time as he would tell it *to a headteacher*. (It doesn't matter whether *B* tells this story as though it happened to himself or to a friend.)

The class can then discuss any differences in words used, tones of voice, gestures, and the general way of acting and speaking in the two situations.

Now work in pairs. Call yourselves *A* and *B*. You will need paper and a pencil.

A should talk to *B* as he would to a good friend. He should describe the most disgusting, slimy and unpleasant monster he can think up. *B* should listen and question to get the details clear in his mind. Then *B* should describe this same monster to *A*, imagining that *A* is *the Queen*.

Discuss between the two of you, and write down, any differences between the words used, tones of voice, gestures and manner on the two occasions.

The whole class can then discuss together the differences people found, using the notes to help. Why are there these differences?
Which sorts of people would you speak to in the same way as you speak to your friends?
Which sorts of people would you speak to in the same way as you would speak to the Queen?